SHORT STORIES ON MY PORCH

Liza Marin

Large print, easy to read

I don't know if it's all because of the amazing lemonade I make for my guests or simply because people need to be listened to with gentleness, but the porch of my house always has guests from the first rays of the sun, and sometimes until late at night.

Many stories are told over glasses filled with the enticing and delicious yellow drink.

Chapter 1

A large carafe of lemonade sits quietly on the veranda table. I squeezed about four lemons, added cold water and a few finely chopped mint leaves. I was going to put it in the fridge. By myself, I can only drink a glass when it's fresh. I want to sit outside for a little longer in the pleasant early summer air. It's 7 p.m. and usually, around this time, someone comes to visit me. That's why I have several glasses ready, on the table next to the lemonade carafe. I love the visits of my neighbors and friends.

I don't even take a sip from my glass when my neighbor and friend Fiona shows up at the gate. I wave my hand at her in greeting. She's in no hurry. She walks slowly from the entrance gate up to my porch.

"I'd love some lemonade," she says when she reaches the porch. "I'm thirsty. You know no one makes lemonade as good as you do. At least not on our street. I might even say in our whole town. You do make the best lemonade here."

"Thank you," I reply. "I've been waiting for you. Help yourself!"

Fiona sits on a chair at the porch table and pours lemonade into a glass. I wait as she savors the refreshing, rich taste.

I know she'll start talking soon. She checks on me often. She is a dear friend. But lately, I feel she's got something she wants to talk about.

"It's very good," says Fiona. "I'll have some more." I see her trying to find the courage to tell me something important.

"How are you, Fiona?" I encourage her to speak.

"Well, fine. Good," she replies. "But I'd be even better if I could talk to my daughter more."

"But don't you talk to her every day? Doesn't she call you?"

"Yes, we talk. But I'd like her to come back and live with us."

"That would mean a long commute in the morning to her new job. You agreed to let her move closer to her job town, didn't you?"

"We agreed, that's true. But now I'm regretting it."

"Your daughter spends a lot of weekends with you, doesn't she?"

"Yes, she does. But it's still not enough. I want to spend more time with her."

"My dear Fiona, I think your daughter has grown up. She's turned into an extraordinary woman. You should trust her."

"I know what you mean. But I feel I'm not a good parent if I don't worry about her."

"Here's what I think. You are great parents because you raised your daughter to be a wonderful person. Now it's time to continue to be good parents by trusting her. She'll be fine."

"So you think it makes us great parents if we let her go?"

"Of course! She'll always come back to you. She's your daughter. But she needs to live on her own and have her own experiences. Believe me, it's for the best."

Fiona took one more sip from the lemonade and then replied with an enormous smile.

"We're wonderful parents, aren't we? That's all that matters. We stand by her in everything she does."

I nod to my neighbor, who relaxes and pours more lemonade into her glass.

"I like your lemonade. I think I'll come over more often. Especially now that my daughter is out of town."

I'm happy that Fiona enjoys coming to visit me. My door is always open to friends and I'll always have a glass of lemonade to share.

Chapter 2

A new summer day, a fresh carafe of lemonade. I wonder who's coming to visit me today. Besides the juice of four lemons, today I added to the lemonade some clementine juice. It has a stronger flavor. Today I will not use mint leaves. I'll leave it with a strong citrus taste and smell.

I took out a jar of syrup for sweetening, to keep close if needed. Who knows what guests I'll have?

I settle into my chair in the soft morning light. I want to rest on the porch for at least an hour before doing a bit of gardening.

I have a lot to do in the garden, but I like to start my day with good lemonade and a chat with a friend or neighbor.

I slowly sip from my glass and lie back on the chair. The chair creaks a little. The noise doesn't bother me. It's like familiar music. It's the sound of relaxation on my porch.

Not a day without visitors. They seem to be drawn to the smell of lemonade and the sound of clinking glasses on my porch table.

I notice the gate of the house swinging and hear a voice from behind.

"Hi. Can you help me get in, please?"

I leave the glass and hurry to the gate. Well, I'm not as quick as I used to be. I gently open the gate and see Adele, the granddaughter of my across-the-street neighbors. She's carrying a small picnic basket, covered.

"Hi, Adele. Come on in. Are you here for lemonade?"

"Grandma sent me to bring you a pie. It's made with cherries from our garden."

Adele is about 12. She's on summer vacation and staying with her grandmother, my neighbor of many years.

"Thank you very much, darling." Adele hands me the pie but doesn't seem to want to go back home.

"Would you like some lemonade?" I ask her. The little girl looks like she wants to talk. She keeps touching her hands and looking out onto the porch.

"Yes, please. Thank you," Adele says and walks confidently to the porch, stepping in front of me. She sits comfortably on one of the two chairs. She looks at me attentively without asking a question until I finish pouring the lemonade.

"It's very tasty," Adele says after sipping. "I need to ask you something. Do you mind?"

"I don't mind. I just hope I can answer you."

"It's easy what I need to ask you. What I have to do is what's hard."

Visibly confused, Adele sips some more of her lemonade. I wait silently for her to find the words or the courage to speak.

"Do you like dogs?" the little girl asks me.

"Yes, very much."

"Why don't you have one here?"

"I had a very nice dog. My daughter took him with her when she moved to another state. He loved her very much and I couldn't keep him here. Why do you ask?"

"Do you think my grandmother loves dogs?"

"I think she does. You can ask her yourself."

"I asked her."

"And?"

"She said she likes them, but they're difficult to care for."

"Yes, that's possible. They depend a lot on humans. They have to be taken care of."

I feel there is a reason behind the girl's questions. But I prefer Adele to say it herself. I don't want to ask her directly.

The little girl has almost finished her glass of lemonade. She's curled up in the deckchair and looks at me as if she wants to say something. I wonder what's bothering her.

She takes a deep, loud breath before putting the glass on the table.

"More lemonade?" I ask.

"No, thank you," Adele replies.

"I have to go. Grandma is waiting for me."

Although she talks about leaving, Adele doesn't get up from her chair. I look at her, smiling. Encouraged, she starts talking.

"If I ask you to put a word for me to Grandma, will you do that?"

Oh, looks like I've become the little girl's ally. But I mustn't disappoint her. *Let's find out more.*

"A word for what?"

"I want a dog of my own."

"So, this is what it's all about? You want a dog?"

"Yes. I really want a dog. I talked to my parents, but we live in an apartment. They told me the dog might get sad not to be free to run around and might feel alone when I'm at school."

"Aha. I understand," I say, waiting for Adele to say more.

"So I thought of this place, here at Grandma's. She has a yard. Grandma's always home and so the dog won't be alone. I just don't know if Grandma wants to take care of my dog."

"Honey, you've already called it my dog. That means you're the one taking care of him. If he stays with Grandma, he'll be Grandma's dog. How do you want it to be?"

"I think I'd want him to be the family dog, but to love me the most. I'll call him Spark."

"Why do you think your grandmother would object?"

"Because she'll need to take care of him. But I can do that, too. I can come here every weekend and on holidays. We don't live far away. It's only an hour's drive."

"But you don't drive."

"Yes, I'll come with my parents. They'll be impressed with my care for the dog, and will take Spark to our apartment occasionally."

"Adele, I heard you. You've said 'care' many times. The entire story revolves around the word 'care'."

"Isn't it about the dog?" Adele asked.

"I think it's about caring and the dog. Actually, about how much you can take care of a dog of your own. That's what you need to talk to your family about."

"And how do I convince them?"

"The best way to gain someone's trust is to show it through actions."

"Well, I don't have a dog to take care of, so how do I show them?"

"Simple. Show your parents and grandparents that you can be responsible. You can start taking care of your flowers and being tidy with your things. Think of any activity around the house or grandma's yard that shows you are serious when you promise something."

"That's simple," Adele rejoiced. "I can take care of Grandma's flowers.

There's a cat sleeping in her loft. I'll feed her. I can even make breakfast sometimes. Lots I can do!" added Adele. With a broad smile, she got up from her chair.

"Would you like some more lemonade?" I asked, but the little girl was already heading for the gate.

"No, thanks. I have to go, I have a lot of work to do," she says, waving her hand goodbye.

I stay there, gently sipping from the tasty lemonade. We may soon have a new dog in the neighborhood. A beautiful, beloved Spark could soon grow up in my neighbor's yard.

Chapter 3

The afternoons on my front porch are always relaxing and peaceful. I love to sit leaning back in my rocking chair, feeling the wind gently blow through the trees near my house. I always have a carafe of lemonade for every moment I want to rest. That's how I feel ready to greet every guest. My lemonade loosens tongues almost every time. Or maybe it's this quiet, relaxing place that makes them open up. I sip a little from the glass, watching as the sky turns reddish, foreshadowing a beautiful sunset.

I hear a motorcycle in the distance. There is no one on our street with a motorcycle. It could be a visitor. The noise stops and I return to my lemonade. I raise my hand above my eyes and look down the street. A young man is approaching my house, pushing a motorcycle with the engine off. I think to myself that it broke down right here on our street. Bad luck. The mechanic's shop is on the other side of town. The young man's got a long way to go. As he gets closer, he waves at me. I get curious and get off the chair. I walk toward the front gate and that's when I recognize my nephew. He takes a few more steps to get next to me.

"Good afternoon," he politely salutes me, as always.

"Hi, Jim. What are you doing with that motorcycle? Is it out of order?"

"No," Jim replies with a sneaky smile on his face. "I just don't want to make any noise. I turned the engine off on the last part of the road. Did you hear it?"

"I heard a little, but vaguely and far away. Why are you asking me about noise?"

"I don't want Grandma to hear it."

"Why? Is it a surprise you're showing up?"

"No, it's not that. I just don't want her to know I came on a motorcycle. She gets upset. She's afraid I could get in an accident. So I'd like to

leave it in your yard and come back later to pick it up. Is that okay?"

"Sure. But what will you tell your grandparents about how you got here?"

"I'll tell them I came by bus, then I walked from the station all the way here."

Jim walks through the gate I opened for him earlier and leaves the motorcycle by the fence. He takes off his leather jacket and hands it to me.

"Can I leave my jacket and helmet with you?"

"Of course," I reply. "And I'll wait for you to show up for lemonade when you come to pick them up."

"Thanks," Jim says, as he steps away. "I think it's going to be late, though. You can leave them on the porch and I'll pick them up without bothering you."

"Not bothered at all," I reply." I'm keen to talk to you and see how you're doing, and how you're getting on with your motorcycle rides. Isn't it hard for you?"

I wanted to ask him how he deals with having to lie to his grandparents every time he comes to visit.

"I can tell you now," Jim replies, slowing down. I can see he wants to talk.

"I love my grandparents very much," he continues. "I want to

come and see them as often as possible and spend as much time with them as possible. I bought my motorcycle because I can get around easily on it. Plus, I like the feeling of freedom it gives me when I ride it. It's my passion."

He looks at me, smiling.

"I somehow have to reconcile my love for my grandparents and my passion for motorcycles. I understand them and try to upset them as little as possible. If I decide to come by motorcycle, I can leave work directly, get here faster, come more often, and spend more time with them. That's how my passion helps me spend more time with my loved ones."

"I'm happy for you, Jim. I'm sure someday soon your grandparents will understand your passion."

"Yes, they do. Grandparents love me, they'll understand."

I wave at him as he slowly walks away toward his grandparents' house. I'll leave a glass of lemonade on the table, next to his jacket and helmet, for him to find when he returns.

Chapter 4

Today I put the last of the lemons in the lemonade. I have to go to the grocery store to get some more. But I'm expecting a package from my daughter and I don't want to be away from home when it arrives.

I've already made friends with Mark, the delivery guy who always comes with packages and I'm glad I saved a few lemons to make him a lemonade.

Usually, the guy arrives around 11. My daughter told me yesterday that I had a package to receive. Mark, the delivery guy, arrives in front of my house right when I'm pouring the lemonade into glasses.

I know he's always in a hurry. He has a lot of packages to deliver, he can't talk to me for long. But he can't resist my lemonade.

"Hi," I hear him greeting me from the gate, holding the package in his arms.

"Hi," I reply. "Come and catch your breath and have some lemonade. I made it, especially for you."

Happy with the invitation, Mark comes in, hands me the package, and sits down on the chair next to the glass of lemonade. Before he sips, he asks me:

"What did you get in the package today?"

"I don't know, Mark, I'm curious too. My daughter wouldn't tell me."

I open the package, which is the size of a painting. Inside I found this week's drawing. My daughter sends me a pencil drawing every week, like a black and white sketch, a self-portrait of herself. She doesn't draw one every week, but most weeks she does.

"I think it's nice that she sends you drawings so often. From what you have told me, she's very talented. What do you have today?"

I unwrap more of the paper and take the drawing out. Mark leans toward me to get a better view.

"It's exquisite. Your daughter's also beautiful and talented."

"I agree."

We both look silently for a few

minutes at the painting showing a young girl tying her hair in a ponytail in front of the mirror. She has gorgeous black hair that contrasts with her white shirt and red lips.

"I have to go," Mark the delivery guy tells me. "I still have packages to deliver. I'll see you soon, next week, right? With another painting, I suppose."

"Yes, I hope I'll have another portrait of hers drawn for me by next week."

"I've been meaning to ask you something for a long time," he says, walking down the stairs to the exit alley. "I was wondering why your daughter doesn't send you pictures of these drawings on your phone. You can always open them, have them close by even when you're not home and near them."

"Yes, that would be easy, of course. But I prefer to have them near me in the house. I display them on the wall one at a time and look at them whenever I pass by. I can even touch them. That way I feel like I have things made by my daughter next to me. When I look at them, it's as if I can see her standing right here in my house, drawing. We see each other often. She visits me whenever she can, but I still miss her. These paintings are extraordinary and make me feel close to her."

"You're lucky," Mark adds before walking out the gate.

"Goodbye," I reply. I know I'll see him again in a week when he will bring me another painting from my talented daughter.

Chapter 5

Today I want to replenish my stock of lemons. I go to the grocery store. When I walk in I see Frank, a neighbor who moved last year on our street.

Frank offers to help me carry the lemons home. He is a talented gardener. We all admire his flower garden. Everyone on the street asks for his advice.

Frank comes into the courtyard with me and leaves the bag of lemons on the porch.

"Thank you so much for your help," I tell him. "If you have time to wait, I'll make some lemonade quickly.

What do you say?" I tempt him to stick around. I'd like to ask him more about the flowers. My garden could look better. Maybe he can teach me a few tricks.

"Sure, I can wait. I'll help you," Frank replies.

"No need, I can manage. You can sit here with me and teach me about the flowers."

I bring out a large carafe of cold water and the lemon squeezer from the house. I start to make the lemonade.

"Your lemonade is famous," Frank says, watching me cut the lemons. "I guess all the neighbors come to you for it, don't they?"

"Well, thanks. And you're famous

for your flower garden. I guess everyone comes to you to admire it, don't they?"

Frank smiles. He has a gentle smile and a gentle face. His hands are big, worn from the garden work.

"Where did you learn to garden?" I ask him.

"That's been my job for 35 years. Now I'm retired."

"And what did you do in that job?"

"I landscaped parks and gardens. I had a company, quite a few employees, and we went everywhere we were needed."

"Don't you miss that? We're a small town here, with only a few gardens."

"I don't work for others anymore,

except for pleasure. I left my son to lead the company. I've retired here to look after the flowers."

"What flowers do you grow the most?"

"Roses. They're my favorites. I think there's a rose for every woman."

I blushed a little and handed him a glass filled with freshly made lemonade.

"Which rose do you think would suit me?" I asked curiously.

"If you have a little patience, I'll come back and get you flowers. I'd like to surprise you."

"Oh, but you mustn't bother."

"It's no trouble at all," Frank replied, getting up from the table on my porch. "I'll be back as soon as I can."

Frank walks away as I sit in my chair. I couldn't refuse him. I think he likes to talk about flowers. Now he's got me curious. I sip my lemonade slowly and look back at the gate, waiting for Frank to return.

Fifteen minutes later, I see him coming. He's holding the flowers behind his back so I can't see what they are. I have to wait until he gets to the porch.

I like roses very much. I like their bright, strong colors. I think they make a beautiful gift for any woman. I wonder what roses Frank's bringing me.

I watch him get close. He holds his hand out in front of him, and a huge bouquet of red roses appears. They're a bright crimson red, part buds and part full bloom.

"Red roses, the color of love, are roses fit for any woman. I hope you like them."

"Ooh Frank, they're wonderful," I reply and my cheeks turn red, just like the roses.

My yellow lemonade makes a delightful contrast on the table next to the red roses.

It's a pleasant evening on my porch. The sunset is rosy; the wind blows gently. The roses are gorgeous. They will look extraordinary in a vase on my table.

I wish I could grow roses like that too. I'll ask Frank, who is a talented gardener, to teach me.

Made in the USA
Monee, IL
20 February 2023

28292899R00033